My Big Sticker Book of Nursery Rhymes

There was an Old Woman
and Other Rhymes

This book belongs to

....

hinkler

COBBLER, COBBLER

Cobbler, cobbler, mend my shoe,
    Have it done by half past two.
Half past two is much too late!
Have it done by half past eight.

OLD KING COLE

Old King Cole
Was a merry old soul,
And a merry old soul was he.
He called for his pipe,
And he called for his bowl,
And he called for his fiddlers three.
Every fiddler, he had a fiddle,
And a very fine fiddle had he;
Twee tweedle dee,
tweedle dee, went the fiddlers.
Oh, there's none so rare,
As can compare
With King Cole and
his fiddlers three.

HUMPTY DUMPTY

Humpty Dumpty sat on a wall,
Humpty Dumpty had a great fall;
All the king's horses and all the king's men
Couldn't put Humpty together again.

HANDY SPANDY

Handy Spandy, Jack-a-dandy,
Loves plum cake and sugar candy.
He bought some at the grocer's shop,
And out he came, hop, hop, hop!

THERE WAS A CROOKED MAN

There was a crooked man, and he went a crooked mile,
He found a crooked sixpence against a crooked stile:
He bought a crooked cat, which caught a crooked mouse,
And they all lived together in a little crooked house.

WEE WILLIE WINKIE

Wee Willie Winkie runs through the town,
Upstairs and downstairs in his nightgown,
Rapping at the window, crying through the lock,
'Are all the children in their beds,
It's past eight o'clock!'

CROSS-PATCH

Cross-patch, draw the latch,
Sit by the fire and spin;
Take a cup, and drink it up,
Then call your neighbours in.

GREGORY GRIGGS

Gregory Griggs, Gregory Griggs,
  Had twenty-seven different wigs.
He wore them up, he wore them down,
To please the people of the town.
He wore them east, he wore them west,
But he never could tell which he loved best.

THERE WAS AN OLD WOMAN WHO LIVED IN A SHOE

There was an old woman
Who lived in a shoe,
She had so many children
She didn't know what to do;
She gave them some broth
Without any bread;
She scolded them soundly
And put them to bed.

COCK A DOODLE DOO

Cock a doodle doo!
My dame has lost her shoe;
My master's lost his fiddling-stick,
And doesn't know what to do.

Cock a doodle doo!
What is my dame to do?
Till master finds his fiddling-stick,
She'll dance without her shoe.

Cock a doodle doo!
My dame has found her shoe,
And master's found his
    fiddling-stick,
Sing doodle doodle doo!

Cock a doodle doo!
My dame will dance with you,
While master fiddles his
    fiddling-stick,
For dame and doodle doo.

Cock a doodle doo!
Dame has lost her shoe;
Gone to bed and scratched her head
And can't tell what to do.

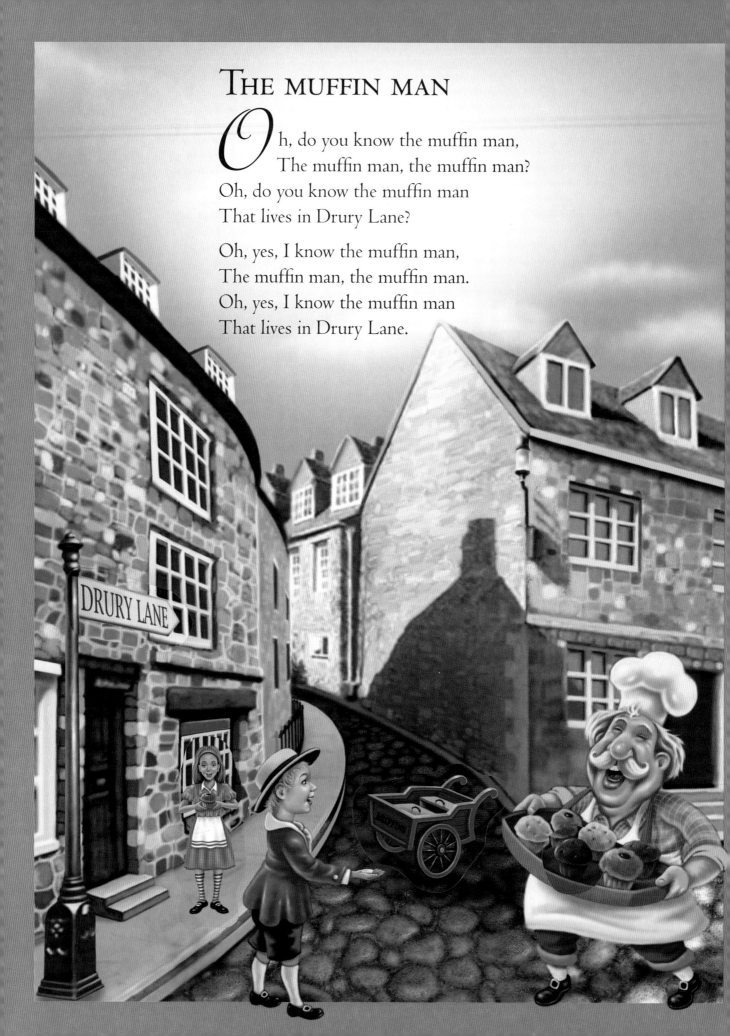

THE MUFFIN MAN

Oh, do you know the muffin man,
The muffin man, the muffin man?
Oh, do you know the muffin man
That lives in Drury Lane?

Oh, yes, I know the muffin man,
The muffin man, the muffin man.
Oh, yes, I know the muffin man
That lives in Drury Lane.

CHAIRS TO MEND

If I'd as much money as I could spend,
    I never would cry, 'Old chairs to mend,
Old chairs to mend! Old chairs to mend!'
I never would cry, 'Old chairs to mend.'

Little Bo-Peep
and Other Rhymes

HEY, DIDDLE, DIDDLE

Hey, diddle, diddle, the cat and the fiddle,
The cow jumped over the moon;
The little dog laughed to see such sport,
And the dish ran away with the spoon.

MONKEYS ON THE BED

Three little monkeys
    Jumping on the bed;
One fell off
And knocked his head.
Momma called the doctor,
The doctor said:
'No more monkeys
Jumping on the bed.'

LITTLE BO-PEEP

Little Bo-Peep has lost her sheep,
And can't tell where to find them;
Leave them alone, and they'll come home,
And bring their tails behind them.

Little Bo-Peep fell fast asleep,
And dreamed she heard them bleating;
But when she awoke she found it a joke,
For they were still a-fleeting.

Then up she took her little crook,
Determined for to find them;
She found them indeed, but it made her heart bleed,
For they'd left their tails behind them.

It happened one day, as Bo-Peep did stray
Into a meadow hard by,
There she spied their tails side by side,
All hung on a tree to dry.

She heaved a sigh, and wiped her eye,
And over the hillocks went rambling,
And tried what she could, as a shepherdess should,
To tack each again to its lambkin.

FOR WANT OF A NAIL

For want of a nail, the shoe was lost;
For want of the shoe, the horse was lost;
For want of the horse, the rider was lost;
For want of the rider, the battle was lost;
For want of the battle, the kingdom was lost;
And all from the want of a horseshoe nail.

GOOSEY, GOOSEY GANDER

Goosey, goosey gander,
    Whither shall I wander?
Upstairs and downstairs
And in my lady's chamber;
There I met an old man
Who would not say his prayers;
I took him by the left leg
And threw him down the stairs.

BAA, BAA, BLACK SHEEP

Baa, baa, black sheep,
Have you any wool?
Yes, sir, yes, sir,
Three bags full;
One for the master,
And one for the dame,
And one for the little boy
Who lives down the lane.

HIGGLETY, PIGGLETY, POP!

Higglety, pigglety, pop!
The dog has eaten the mop;
The pig's in a hurry,
The cat's in a flurry,
Higglety, pigglety, pop!

I HAD A LITTLE HEN

I had a little hen,
    The prettiest ever seen;
She washed up the dishes,
And kept the house clean.
She went to the mill
To fetch me some flour,
She brought it home
In less than an hour.
She baked me my bread,
She brewed me my ale,
She sat by the fire
And told many a fine tale.

GREY GOOSE AND GANDER

Grey goose and gander
    Waft your wings together,
And carry the good king's daughter
Over the one-strand river.

MARY HAD A LITTLE LAMB

Mary had a little lamb,
Its fleece was white as snow;
And everywhere that Mary went
The lamb was sure to go.

It followed her to school one day,
Which was against the rule;
It made the children laugh and play
To see a lamb at school.

And so the teacher turned it out,
But still it lingered near,
And waited patiently about
Till Mary did appear.

'What makes the lamb love Mary so?'
The eager children cry;
'Why, Mary loves the lamb, you know,'
The teacher did reply.

SIX LITTLE MICE

Six little mice sat down to spin,
  Pussy passed by, and she peeped in.
What are you doing, my little men?
Weaving coats for gentlemen.
Shall I come in and cut off your threads?
No, no, Mistress Pussy, you'd bite off our heads!
Oh, no, I won't, I'll help you to spin.
That may be so, but you can't come in!

HICKETY, PICKETY

Hickety, pickety, my black hen,
　　She lays eggs for gentlemen;
Gentlemen come every day
To see what my black hen doth lay;
Sometimes nine and sometimes ten,
Hickety, pickety, my black hen.

Man in the Moon

and Other Rhymes

ROCK-A-BYE, BABY, ON THE TREE TOP

Rock-a-bye, baby, on the tree top,
When the wind blows, the cradle will rock;
When the bough breaks, the cradle will fall,
Down will come baby, cradle and all.

DANCE, LITTLE BABY

Dance, little baby, dance up high!
Never mind, baby, Mother is by.
Crow and caper, caper and crow,
There, little baby, there you go.
Up to the ceiling, down to the ground,
Backwards and forwards, round and round!
Dance, little baby, and Mother shall sing,
With the merry chorus, ding-a-ding, ding.

SLEEP, BABY, SLEEP

Sleep, baby, sleep,
    Thy father guards the sheep,
Thy mother shakes the dreamland tree,
And from it fall sweet dreams for thee.
Sleep, baby, sleep.

Sleep, baby, sleep,
Our cottage vale is deep.
The little lamb is on the green,
With woolly fleece so soft and clean.
Sleep, baby, sleep.

Sleep, baby, sleep,
Down where the woodbines creep.
Be always like the lamb so mild,
A kind and sweet and gentle child.
Sleep, baby, sleep.

ALL THE PRETTY LITTLE HORSES

Hush-a-bye, don't you cry
Go to sleep, little baby.
When you wake
You shall have
All the pretty little horses,
Blacks and bays,
Dapples and greys,
Coach and six white horses.

Hush-a-bye, don't you cry,
Go to sleep, little baby.
When you wake
You shall have cake
And all the pretty little horses.

THE MAN IN THE MOON

The man in the moon looked out of the moon,
  And this is what he said:
'Now that I'm getting up, 'tis time
All children went to bed!'

Hush, the Waves Are Rolling In

Hush, the waves are rolling in,
   White with foam, white with foam,
Father toils amid the din,
While baby sleeps at home.

Hush, the ship rides in the gale,
   Where they roam, where they roam,
Father seeks the roving whale,
While baby sleeps at home.

Hush, the wind sweeps o'er the deep,
   All alone, all alone,
Mother now the watch will keep,
Till father's ship comes home.

BYE, BABY BUNTING

Bye, baby bunting,
    Daddy's gone a-hunting,
To fetch a little rabbit skin
To wrap his baby bunting in.

HUSH, LITTLE BABY

Hush, little baby, don't say a word,
Papa's going to buy you a mocking bird.

If that mocking bird won't sing,
Papa's going to buy you a diamond ring.

If that diamond ring turns brass,
Papa's going to buy you a looking glass.

If that looking glass gets broke,
Papa's going to buy you a billy goat.

If that billy goat won't pull,
Papa's going to buy you a cart and bull.

If that cart and bull turn over,
Papa's going to buy you a dog named Rover.

If that dog named Rover won't bark,
Papa's going to buy you a horse and cart.

If that horse and cart fall down,
You'll still be the sweetest little baby in town.

COME TO THE WINDOW

Come to the window,
  My baby, with me,
And look at the stars
That shine on the sea!
There are two little stars
That play at bo-peep
With two little fishes
Far down in the deep.
And two little frogs
Cry, 'Neap, neap, neap,
I see a dear baby
That should be asleep!'

ROCK-A-BYE, BABY, THY CRADLE IS GREEN

Rock-a-bye, baby, thy cradle is green,
Father's a nobleman, Mother's a queen.
And Betty's a lady and wears a gold ring,
And Johnny's a drummer and drums for the king.

BRAHMS' LULLABY

*L*ullaby and goodnight,
With roses bestride,
With lilies bedecked,
'Neath baby's sweet bed.

May thou sleep, may thou rest,
May thy slumber be blest.
May thou sleep, may thou rest,
May thy slumber be blest.

Lullaby and goodnight,
Thy mother's delight.
Bright angels around,
My darling, shall guard.

They will guide thee from harm,
Thou art safe in my arms.
They will guide thee from harm,
Thou art safe in my arms.

Johannes Brahms

Sing a Song of Sixpence
and Other Rhymes

POLLY PUT THE KETTLE ON

Polly, put the kettle on,
        Polly, put the kettle on,
Polly, put the kettle on,
We'll all have tea.

Sukey, take it off again,
Sukey, take it off again,
Sukey, take it off again,
They've all gone away.

LITTLE JACK HORNER

Little Jack Horner
Sat in a corner,
Eating a Christmas pie;
He put in his thumb,
And pulled out a plum,
And said, 'What a
good boy am I!'

SING A SONG OF SIXPENCE

*S*ing a song of sixpence,
  A pocket full of rye;
Four and twenty blackbirds
Baked in a pie.

When the pie was opened
The birds began to sing;
Wasn't that a dainty dish
To set before the king?

The king was in his counting-house
Counting out his money;
The queen was in the parlour
Eating bread and honey.

The maid was in the garden
Hanging out the clothes,
When down came a blackbird,
And pecked off her nose.

JELLY ON A PLATE

Jelly on a plate,
Jelly on a plate,
Wibble, wobble, wibble, wobble,
Jelly on a plate.

THE GINGERBREAD MAN

Smiling girls, rosy boys,
　Come and buy my little toys.
Monkeys made of gingerbread
And sugar horses painted red.

PEASE PORRIDGE HOT

Pease porridge hot,
   Pease porridge cold,
Pease porridge in the pot,
Nine days old.

Some like it hot,
Some like it cold,
Some like it in the pot,
Nine days old.

PETER PIPER

Peter Piper picked a peck of pickled peppers;
A peck of pickled peppers Peter Piper picked;
If Peter Piper picked a peck of pickled peppers,
Where's the peck of pickled peppers Peter Piper picked?

Hot cross buns!
Hot cross buns!
One a penny, two a penny,
Hot cross buns!

If you have no daughters,
Give them to your sons.
One a penny, two a penny,
Hot cross buns!

BETTY BOTTER

Betty Botter bought some butter,
But, she said, the butter's bitter;
If I put it in my batter
It will make my batter bitter,
But a bit of better butter
That would make my batter better.
So she bought a bit of butter
Better than her bitter butter,
And she put it in her batter
And the batter was not bitter.
So 'twas better Betty Botter
Bought a bit of better butter.

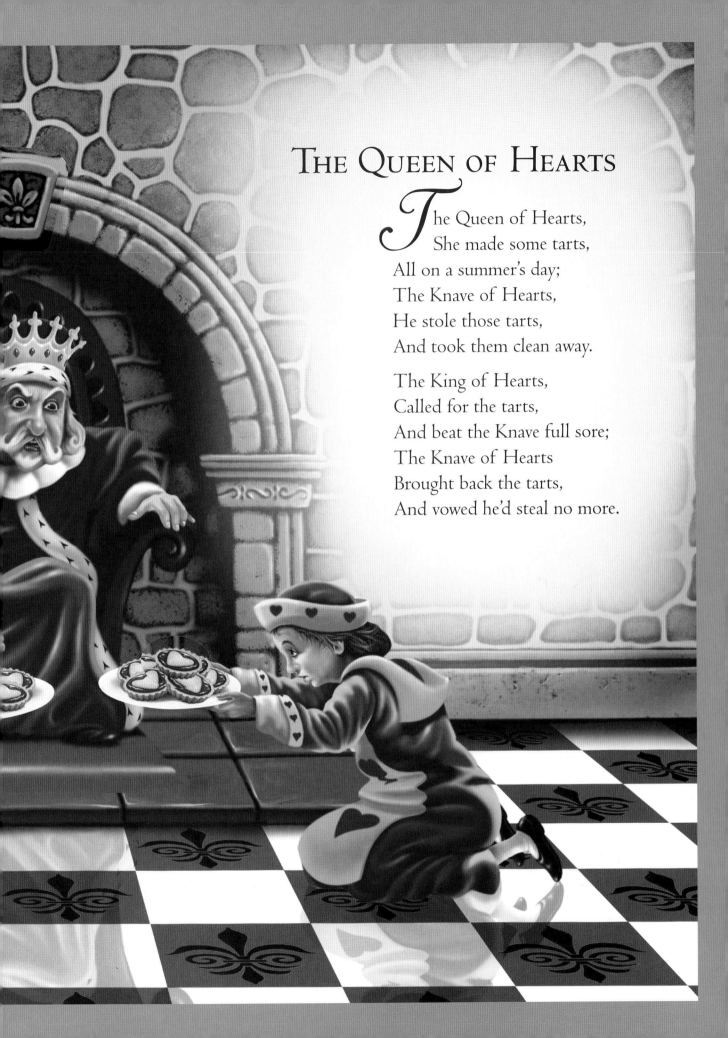

THE QUEEN OF HEARTS

The Queen of Hearts,
  She made some tarts,
All on a summer's day;
The Knave of Hearts,
He stole those tarts,
And took them clean away.

The King of Hearts,
Called for the tarts,
And beat the Knave full sore;
The Knave of Hearts
Brought back the tarts,
And vowed he'd steal no more.

Jack Sprat

Jack Sprat could eat no fat,
His wife could eat no lean,
And so between them both, you see,
They licked the platter clean.

IF ALL THE WORLD WAS APPLE PIE

If all the world was apple pie,

And all the sea was ink,

And all the trees were bread and cheese,

What should we have to drink?

Jack and Jill
and Other Rhymes

GIRLS AND BOYS, COME OUT TO PLAY

Girls and boys, come out to play,
 The moon doth shine as bright as day.
Leave your supper and leave your sleep,
And join your playfellows into the street.
Come with a whoop and come with a call,
Come with a good will or not at all.
Up the ladder and down the wall,
A half-penny loaf will serve us all;
You find milk and I'll find flour,
And we'll have a pudding in half an hour.

LITTLE BOY BLUE

Little Boy Blue,
Come blow your horn,
The sheep's in the meadow,
The cow's in the corn.

Where is the boy
Who looks after the sheep?
He's under the haystack,
Fast asleep.

Will you wake him?
No, not I,
For if I do,
He's sure to cry.

ELSIE MARLEY

Elsie Marley is grown so fine,
She won't get up to feed the swine,
But lies in bed till eight or nine,
And surely she does take her time.

MOTION

Fishes swim in waters clear,
Birds fly up into the air,
Serpents creep along the ground,
Boys and girls run round and round.

JACK, BE NIMBLE

Jack, be nimble,
Jack, be quick,
Jack, jump over
The candlestick.

JACK AND JILL

Jack and Jill went up the hill
To fetch a pail of water;
Jack fell down and broke his crown,
And Jill came tumbling after.

Then up Jack got and home did trot
As fast as he could caper;
He went to bed to mend his head
With vinegar and brown paper.

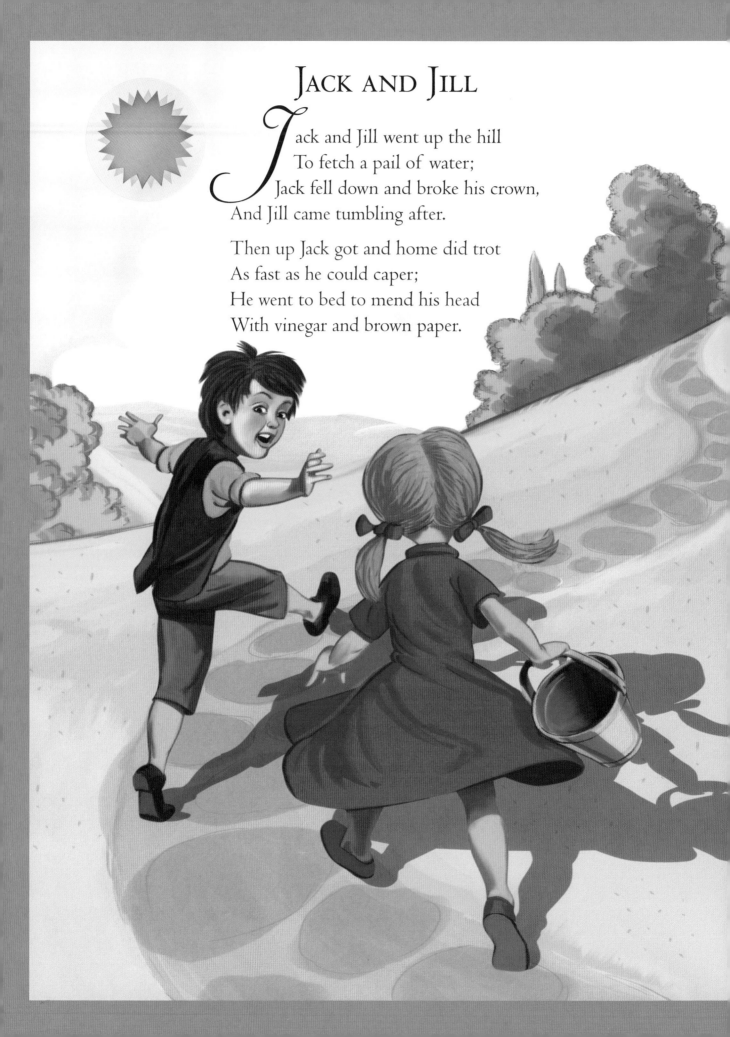

SALLY, GO ROUND THE SUN

*S*ally, go round the sun,
  Sally, go round the moon,
Sally, go round the chimneypots,
On a Saturday afternoon.

TWEEDLEDUM AND TWEEDLEDEE

Tweedledum and Tweedledee
    Agreed to fight a battle,
For Tweedledum said Tweedledee
Had spoilt his nice new rattle.
Just then flew by a monstrous crow
As big as a tar barrel,
Which frightened both the heroes so,
They quite forgot their quarrel.

WHAT ARE LITTLE BOYS MADE OF?

What are little boys made of, made of?
    What are little boys made of?
Frogs and snails and puppy dogs' tails,
That's what little boys are made of.

What are little girls made of, made of?
What are little girls made of?
Sugar and spice and all things nice,
That's what little girls are made of.

PUPPY
DOGS' TAILS

Spice

SUGAR SPICE

WASH THE DISHES

Wash the dishes, wipe the dishes,
  Ring the bell for tea.
Three good wishes, three good kisses,
I will give to thee.

DIDDLE, DIDDLE, DUMPLING, MY SON JOHN

Diddle, diddle, dumpling, my son John,
   Went to bed with his trousers on;
One shoe off, and one shoe on,
Diddle, diddle, dumpling, my son John.

Hickory, Dickory, Dock
and Other Rhymes

LITTLE MISS MUFFET

Little Miss Muffet
Sat on a tuffet,
Eating her curds and whey;
Along came a spider,
Who sat down beside her
And frightened Miss
   Muffet away.

HICKORY, DICKORY, DOCK

Hickory, dickory, dock,
The mouse ran up the clock,
The clock struck one,
The mouse ran down,
Hickory, dickory, dock.

THE DOVE SAYS, 'COO, COO'

The dove says, 'Coo, coo, what shall I do?
I can scarce maintain two.'
'Pooh! Pooh!' says the wren; 'I have got ten,
And keep them all like gentlemen.'

TWO CATS OF KILKENNY

There once were two cats of Kilkenny,
  Each thought there was one cat too many.
So they fought and they fit,
And they scratched and they bit,
Till, excepting their nails,
And the tips of their tails,
Instead of two cats, there weren't any.

WHAT DO YOU SUPPOSE?

What do you suppose?
A bee sat on my nose!

Then what do you think?
He gave me a wink.

And said, 'I beg your pardon,
I thought you were the garden!'

HARK, HARK, THE DOGS DO BARK

Hark, hark, the dogs do bark,
  The beggars are coming to town:
Some in rags, and some in jags,
And one in a velvet gown.

THREE LITTLE KITTENS

Three little kittens, they lost their mittens
  And they began to cry;
Oh, mother dear, we sadly fear
That we have lost our mittens.
What! Lost your mittens, you naughty kittens!
Then you shall have no pie.
Mee-ow, mee-ow, mee-ow,
No, you shall have no pie.

Three little kittens, they found their mittens,
And they began to cry;
Oh, mother dear, see here, see here,
For we have found our mittens.
Put on your mittens, you silly kittens,
And you shall have some pie.
Purr-r, purr-r, purr-r,
Oh, let us have some pie.

Three little kittens put on their mittens,
And soon ate up the pie;
Oh, mother dear, we greatly fear
That we have soiled our mittens.
What! Soiled your mittens, you naughty kittens!
Then they began to sigh,
Mee-ow, mee-ow, mee-ow,
Then they began to sigh.

The three little kittens, they washed their mittens,
And hung them out to dry;
Oh, mother dear, do you not hear
That we have washed our mittens?
What! Washed your mittens, you good little kittens,
But I smell a rat close by.
Mee-ow, mee-ow, mee-ow,
We smell a rat close by.

DING DONG BELL

Ding dong bell,
    Pussy's in the well.
Who put her in?
Little Johnny Green.
Who pulled her out?
Little Tommy Stout.
What a naughty boy was that,
To try to drown poor pussy cat,
Who never did him any harm,
But killed the mice in his father's barn.

LITTLE BIRD

Once I saw a little bird
    Come hop, hop, hop.
So I cried, 'Little bird,
Will you stop, stop, stop?'

I was going to the window
To say, 'How do you do?'
But he shook his little tail,
And far away he flew.

THE NORTH WIND DOTH BLOW

The north wind doth blow,
    And we shall have snow,
And what will poor Robin do then,
Poor thing?

He'll sit in a barn,
And keep himself warm,
And hide his head under his wing,
Poor thing.

The north wind doth blow,
And we shall have snow,
And what shall the honey-bee do,
Poor thing?

In his hive he will stay
Till the cold's passed away,
And then he'll come out in the spring,
Poor thing.

The north wind doth blow,
And we shall have snow,
And what will the dormouse do then,
Poor thing?

Rolled up like a ball
In his nest snug and small,
He'll sleep till warm weather comes back,
Poor thing.

The north wind doth blow,
And we shall have snow,
And what will the children do then,
Poor things?

When lessons are done,
They'll jump, skip and run,
And that's how they'll keep themselves warm,
Poor things.

OH WHERE, OH WHERE, HAS MY LITTLE DOG GONE?

Oh where, oh where,
Has my little dog gone?
Oh where, oh where can he be?

With his ears cut short
And his tail cut long,
Oh where, oh where is he?

LADYBIRD, LADYBIRD

Ladybird, ladybird, fly away home,
Your house is on fire, your children are gone;
All but one, and her name is Ann,
And she crept under the pudding pan.

Five Little Ducks

and Other Rhymes

THREE ELEPHANTS

One elephant went out to play
    Upon a spider's web one day.
He thought it such a tremendous stunt
That he called for another little elephant.

Two elephants went out to play
Upon a spider's web one day.
They thought it such a tremendous stunt
That they called for another little elephant.

Three elephants went out to play
Upon a spider's web one day.
The web went creak,
    the web went crack
And all of a sudden,
    they all ran back.

ONE FOR SORROW, TWO FOR JOY

One for sorrow, two for joy,
Three for a girl and four for a boy,
Five for silver, six for gold,
Seven for a secret never to be told,
Eight for a letter over the sea,
Nine for a lover as true as can be.

THIRTY DAYS HATH SEPTEMBER

Thirty days hath September,
April, June and November;
February has twenty-eight alone,
All the rest have thirty-one,
Excepting leap-year – that's the time,
When February's days are twenty-nine.

CHOOK, CHOOK, CHOOK

Chook, chook, chook-chook-chook,
Good morning, Mrs Hen,
How many chickens have you got?
Madam, I've got ten.

Four of them are yellow,
And four of them are brown,
And two of them are speckled red,
The nicest in the town.

ONE, TWO, BUCKLE MY SHOE

*O*ne, two, buckle my shoe;

Three, four, knock on the door;

Five, six, pick up sticks;

Seven, eight, lay them straight;

Nine, ten, a good fat hen.

Eleven, twelve, dig and delve;

Thirteen, fourteen, maids a-courting;

Fifteen, sixteen, maids in the kitchen;

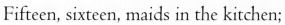

Seventeen, eighteen, maids a-waiting;

Nineteen, twenty, my plate's empty.

FIVE LITTLE DUCKS

Five little ducks went out one day
  Over the hills and far away.
Mother duck said, 'Quack quack, quack quack!'
But only four little ducks came back.

Four little ducks went out one day
Over the hills and far away.
Mother duck said, 'Quack quack, quack quack!'
But only three little ducks came back.

Three little ducks went out one day
Over the hills and far away.
Mother duck said, 'Quack quack, quack quack!'
But only two little ducks came back.

Two little ducks went out one day
Over the hills and far away.
Mother duck said, 'Quack quack, quack quack!'
But only one little duck came back.

One little duck went out one day
Over the hills and far away.
Mother duck said, 'Quack quack, quack quack!'
But none of those five little ducks came back.

Mother duck she went out one day
Over the hills and far away.
Mother duck said, 'Quack quack, quack quack!'
And all of those five little ducks came back.

ONE, TWO, THREE, FOUR, FIVE

One, two, three, four, five,
    Once I caught a fish alive;
Six, seven, eight, nine, ten,
Then I let it go again.

Why did you let it go?
Because it bit my finger so.
Which finger did it bite?
This little finger on the right.

HERE IS THE BEEHIVE

Here is the beehive,
But where are all the bees?
Hiding away where nobody sees.

Here they come creeping
Out of their hive,
One and two and three, four, five.

THREE JELLYFISH

Three jellyfish, three jellyfish,
  Three jellyfish, sitting on a rock.
One fell off! ... Ooooh ... Splash!

Two jellyfish, two jellyfish,
Two jellyfish, sitting on a rock.
One fell off! ... Ooooh ... Splash!

One jellyfish, one jellyfish,
One jellyfish, sitting on a rock.
One fell off! ... Ooooh ... Splash!

No jellyfish, no jellyfish,
No jellyfish, sitting on a rock.
One jumped up! ... Hooray!

One jellyfish, one jellyfish,
One jellyfish, sitting on a rock.
One jumped up! ... Hooray!

Two jellyfish, two jellyfish,
Two jellyfish, sitting on a rock.
One jumped up! ... Hooray!

Three jellyfish, three jellyfish,
Three jellyfish, sitting on a rock.
One fell off! ... Ooooh ... Splash!

Row, Row, Row Your Boat
and Other Rhymes

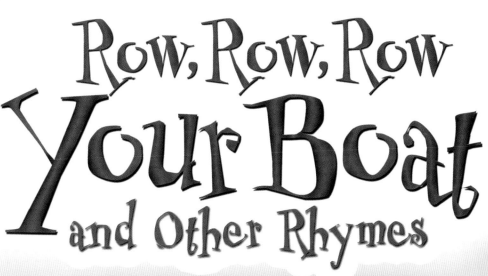

RUB-A-DUB DUB

Rub-a-dub dub,
Three men in a tub,
And who do you think they be?
The butcher, the baker,
The candlestick-maker,
Turn them out, knaves all three.

THE FLYING PIG

Dickery, dickery, dare,
  The pig flew up in the air;
The man in brown
Soon brought him down.
Dickery, dickery, dare.

I SAW A SHIP A-SAILING

I saw a ship a-sailing,
   A-sailing on the sea;
And oh! It was laden
With pretty things for me.

There were comfits in the cabin,
And apples in the hold;
The sails were made of silk,
And the masts were made of gold.

The four-and-twenty sailors
That stood between the decks,
Were four-and-twenty white mice,
With chains about their necks.

The captain was a duck,
With a packet on his back,
And when the ship began to move,
The captain said, 'Quack, quack!'

PUSSYCAT, PUSSYCAT

Pussycat, pussycat, where have you been?
    I've been to London to visit the queen.
Pussycat, pussycat, what did you there?
I frightened a little mouse under her chair.

ROW, ROW, ROW YOUR BOAT

Row, row, row your boat,
Gently down the stream,
Merrily, merrily, merrily, merrily,
Life is but a dream.

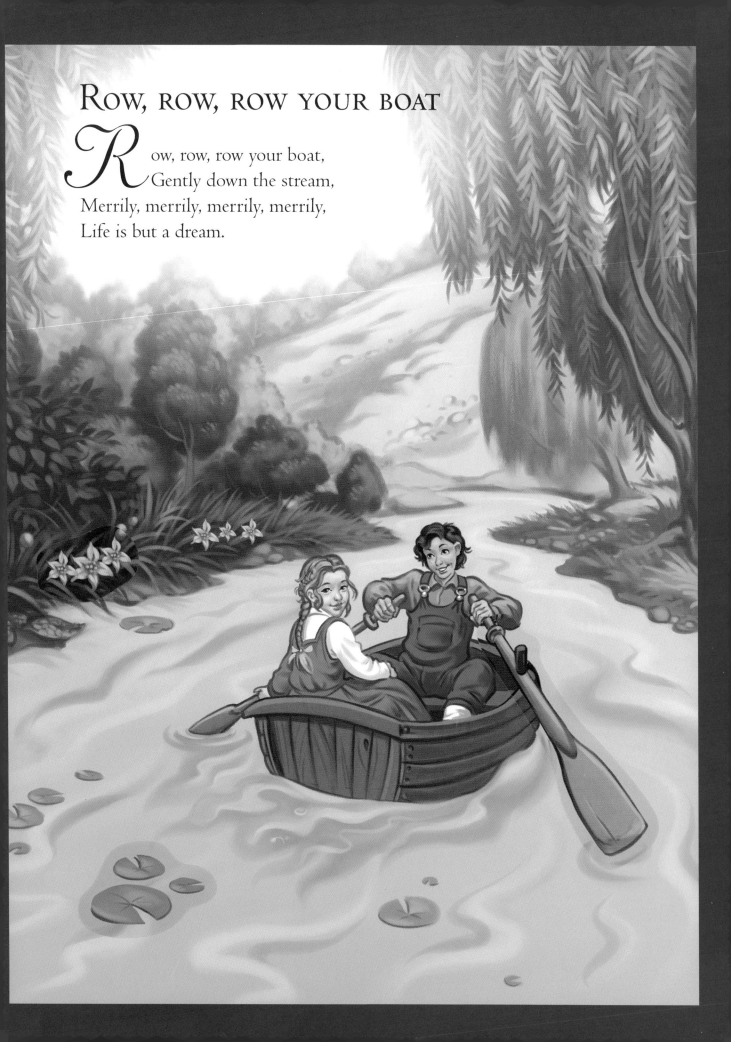

As I was going to St Ives

As I was going to St Ives,
I met a man with seven wives.
Each wife had seven sacks.
Each sack had seven cats.
Each cat had seven kits.
Kits, cats, sacks and wives:
How many were going to St Ives?

DOCTOR FOSTER

Doctor Foster went to Gloucester
In a shower of rain;
He stepped in a puddle,
Right up to his middle,
And never went there again.

THERE WAS
AN OLD WOMAN

There was an old woman tossed up in a basket
    Seventeen times as high as the moon;
Where she was going, I couldn't but ask it,
For in her hand she carried a broom.

'Old woman, old woman, old woman,' quoth I,
'O wither, O wither, O wither, so high?'
'To sweep the cobwebs from the sky!'
'Shall I go with thee?'
'Aye, by-and-by.'

How many miles to Babylon?

How many miles to Babylon?
    Three score miles and ten.
Can I get there by candlelight?
Yes, and back again.
If your heels be nimble and light,
You may get there by candlelight.

I SAW THREE SHIPS

I saw three ships come sailing by,
Come sailing by, come sailing by,
I saw three ships come sailing by,
On Christmas Day in the morning.

And what do you think was in them then,
Was in them then, was in them then?
And what do you think was in them then,
On Christmas Day in the morning?

Three pretty girls were in them then,
Were in them then, were in them then,
Three pretty girls were in them then,
On Christmas Day in the morning.

One could whistle, and one could sing,
And one could play on the violin;
So joy there was at my wedding,
On Christmas Day in the morning.

LITTLE GIRL, LITTLE GIRL

Little girl, little girl, where have you been?
Gathering roses to give to the queen.
Little girl, little girl, what gave she you?
She gave me a diamond as big as my shoe.

THE MAN IN
THE MOON

The man in the moon,
  Came tumbling down,
And asked his way to Norwich.
He went by the south,
And burnt his mouth
With supping cold pease-porridge.

Published by Hinkler Books Pty Ltd
45–55 Fairchild Street
Heatherton Victoria 3202 Australia
www.hinkler.com.au

hinkler

© Hinkler Books Pty Ltd 2006

Illustrations: Andrew Hopgood, Melissa Webb,
Gerad Taylor, Geoff Cook and Anton Petrov
Design: Sonia Dixon Design
Art direction: Silvana Paolini
Cover design: Katy Wall
Prepress: Graphic Print Group

ISBN: 978 1 7418 1251 0

Printed and bound in Malaysia